# LET'S GO, FROGGY!

LIBREX

# LET'S GO, FROGGY!

by JONATHAN LONDON
illustrated by FRANK REMKIEWICZ

PUFFIN BOOKS

For Maureen and Grandma "Cook,"
who know "where it's at," and for
Sean and Aaron, who sometimes don't

With special appreciation to my
great aunt Norma Jacobson—
her joie de vivre
—J. L.

For Grace
—F.R.

PUFFIN BOOKS
Published by the Penguin Group
Penguin Books Ltd, 27 Wrights Lane, London W8 5TZ, England
Penguin Books USA Inc., 375 Hudson Street, New York, New York 10014, U.S.A.
Penguin Books Australia Ltd, Ringwood, Victoria, Australia
Penguin Books Canada Ltd, 10 Alcorn Avenue, Toronto, Ontario, Canada M4V 3B2
Penguin Books (N.Z.) Ltd, 182-190 Wairau Road, Auckland 10, New Zealand

Penguin Books Ltd, Registered Offices: Harmondsworth, Middlesex, England

First published in the United States of America by Viking,
a division of Penguin Books USA Inc. 1994
Published in Puffin Books 1996

10 9 8 7 6 5 4 3 2 1

Text copyright © Jonathan London, 1994
Illustrations copyright © Frank Remkiewicz, 1994
All rights reserved
ISBN 0-14-055972-8

Printed in the United States of America

It was warm.
Froggy woke up
and looked out of the window.
Birds, butterflies, flowers.
"Hurray!" sang Froggy.
"I want to go out and play!"

"Okay," said his father.
"How about a bike trip
 and a picnic?
 Would you like that?"

"Yes!" cried Froggy. "Let's go!"

"First you have to get ready, silly,"
said his father.

"Okay!" said Froggy. "I'm getting ready!"

So Froggy got dressed.

He pulled on his underwear—*zap!*

Pulled on his shorts—*zip!*

Pulled on his socks—*zoop!*

Pulled on his sneakers—*zup!*

And buttoned up his shirt—*zut! zut! zut!*

FRRROOGGYY!

called his father. "Let's go!"
**"I'm re-e-a-d-y!"** yelled Froggy
and flopped out to
show him—*flop flop flop.*

"But Froggy!" said his father.

"You need your bicycle helmet!"

"I don't know where it is!" said Froggy.

"It's wherever you left it!"

"I forget!"

"You have to *look* for it!"

So Froggy looked for his helmet.

He looked under the sink—*bonk!*

He looked in the fridge—*slam!*

He looked in his toy chest.

"I found it!" yelled Froggy

and put it on with a slap—*zat!*

FRRROOGGYY!

called his father. "Let's go!"

**"I'm re-e-a-d-y!"** yelled Froggy—*flop flop flop.*

"You should bring your butterfly net!"
said his father.
"I don't know where it is!"
"It's wherever you left it!"

So Froggy looked for

his butterfly net.

He looked under the coffee table—*bonk!*

He looked in the rubbish bin—*slam!*

He looked in his father's golf bag.

"I found it!" yelled Froggy

and swung it at a fly—*swish!*—

but missed.

FRRROOGGYY!

called his father. "Let's go!"

**"I'm re-e-a-d-y!"** yelled Froggy—*flop flop flop.*

"How about the ball Grandpapa gave you?"
 asked his father.
"I don't know where it is!"
"It's wherever you left it!"

So Froggy looked for his ball.

He looked under the cooker—*bonk!*

He looked in the cookie jar—*slam!*

He looked in the bath.

"I found it!" he yelled

and kicked it into the goldfish bowl—*splash!*

FRRROOGGYY!

called his father. "Let's go!"
**"I'm re-e-a-d-y!"** yelled Froggy—*flop flop flop.*

"Let's bring the bag of peaches
 Auntie Loulou gave you," said his father.
"I don't know where it is!"
"It's wherever you left it!"

So Froggy looked for the

bag of peaches.

He looked under the kitchen table—*bonk!*

He looked in his wardrobe—*slam!*

He looked in his bed.

"I found it!" yelled Froggy

and took a bite—*scrunch!*

(He was getting hungry.)

**FRRROOGGYY!**

called his father. "Let's go!"

"**I'm re-e-a-d-y!**" yelled Froggy—*flop flop flop.*

"Daddy, can I bring that pack of trading cards Uncle Gerard gave me?"

"Okay, Froggy, but hurry. Let's go!"

"I don't know where it is!"

"It's wherever you left it!"

"*Oops!* Here it is! I found it!
It was in my pocket!
Can we go now, Daddy? I'm *ready!*"

"Okay, but do you know
where my red backpack is?" asked his father.

"Daddy! *It's wherever you left it!*"

"I forget!"
Froggy pointed.

# IT'S ON YOUR BACK!

Froggy laughed.
"Oops!" cried Froggy's father,
looking more red in the face than green.

Ready to go at last, Froggy flopped over
to the bicycle—*flop flop flop.*

"Let's go, Froggy!" said his father.

"I'm *hungry!*" said Froggy.

"I want to eat NOW!"

So they ate their picnic
on the patio—*munch scrunch munch.*

"Okay, I'm ready!" said Froggy.
"Let's go!" said his father.

And off they pedalled into the sunset—*wee!*